SNOW WHITE

The Classic Edition

by the Brothers Grimm ✳ Illustrated by Charles Santore

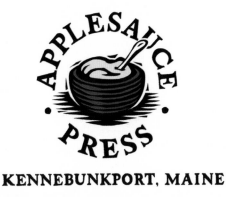

KENNEBUNKPORT, MAINE

Applesauce Press is an imprint of
Cider Mill Press Book Publishers
"Where good books are ready for press"
PO Box 454
12 Spring Street
Kennebunkport, Maine 04046
Visit us online! www.cidermillpress.com

Typography: ITC Caslon 224, Serlio

Printed in China
1 2 3 4 5 6 7 8 9 0
First Edition

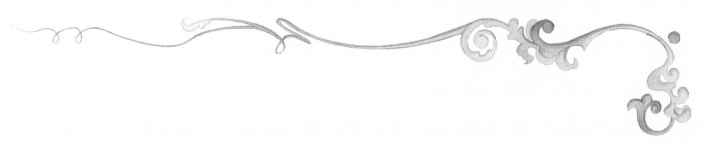

This book is dedicated to the first Charles Santore in our family, my father.

—Charles Santore

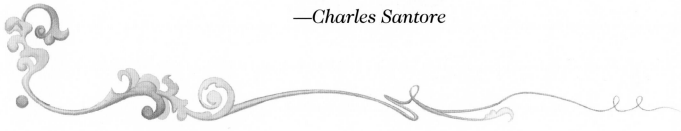

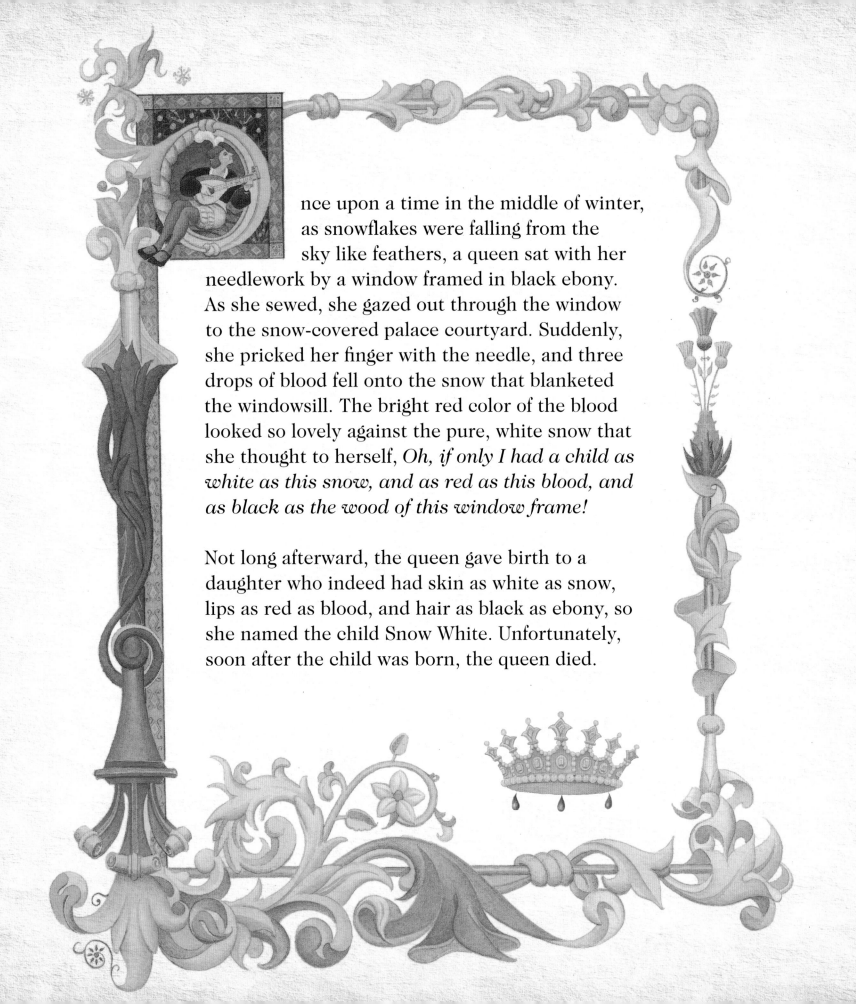

nce upon a time in the middle of winter, as snowflakes were falling from the sky like feathers, a queen sat with her needlework by a window framed in black ebony. As she sewed, she gazed out through the window to the snow-covered palace courtyard. Suddenly, she pricked her finger with the needle, and three drops of blood fell onto the snow that blanketed the windowsill. The bright red color of the blood looked so lovely against the pure, white snow that she thought to herself, *Oh, if only I had a child as white as this snow, and as red as this blood, and as black as the wood of this window frame!*

Not long afterward, the queen gave birth to a daughter who indeed had skin as white as snow, lips as red as blood, and hair as black as ebony, so she named the child Snow White. Unfortunately, soon after the child was born, the queen died.

After a year had gone by, the king married another woman. The new queen was a very handsome woman, but was so proud of her looks that she could not bear for anyone to surpass her in beauty. She possessed a magic mirror, and every day she gazed upon her reflection in the glass, saying,

"Mirror, mirror on the wall, Who is fairest of us all?"

The mirror would answer, *"Queen, you are the fairest of them all."*

Then she was pleased, for she knew that the mirror always spoke the truth.

But as little Snow White grew up, she became prettier and prettier, and by the time she was seven years old, she was as lovely as a sunny day, and even more beautiful than the queen herself.

One day when the queen asked the mirror,
"Mirror, mirror on the wall,
  Who is fairest of us all?"
The mirror replied,
  "The queen was fairest yesterday,
  But Snow White is fairer now, they say."
This answer so angered the Queen that
she became green with envy. From that
hour, her heart turned against Snow
White, and she hated the innocent
little girl.

$\mathcal{P}$ride and envy grew in the queen's heart like a weed, so that she had no rest, day or night. At last she sent for a huntsman and said, "Take the child into the woods. You must kill her, and bring me her heart as proof she is dead."

The huntsman obeyed the queen and took Snow White out into the forest, but when he drew his hunting knife to pierce her innocent heart, she began to cry.

"Oh, dear huntsman, please spare my life," she pleaded, "and I will run away into the wild forest and never come home again."

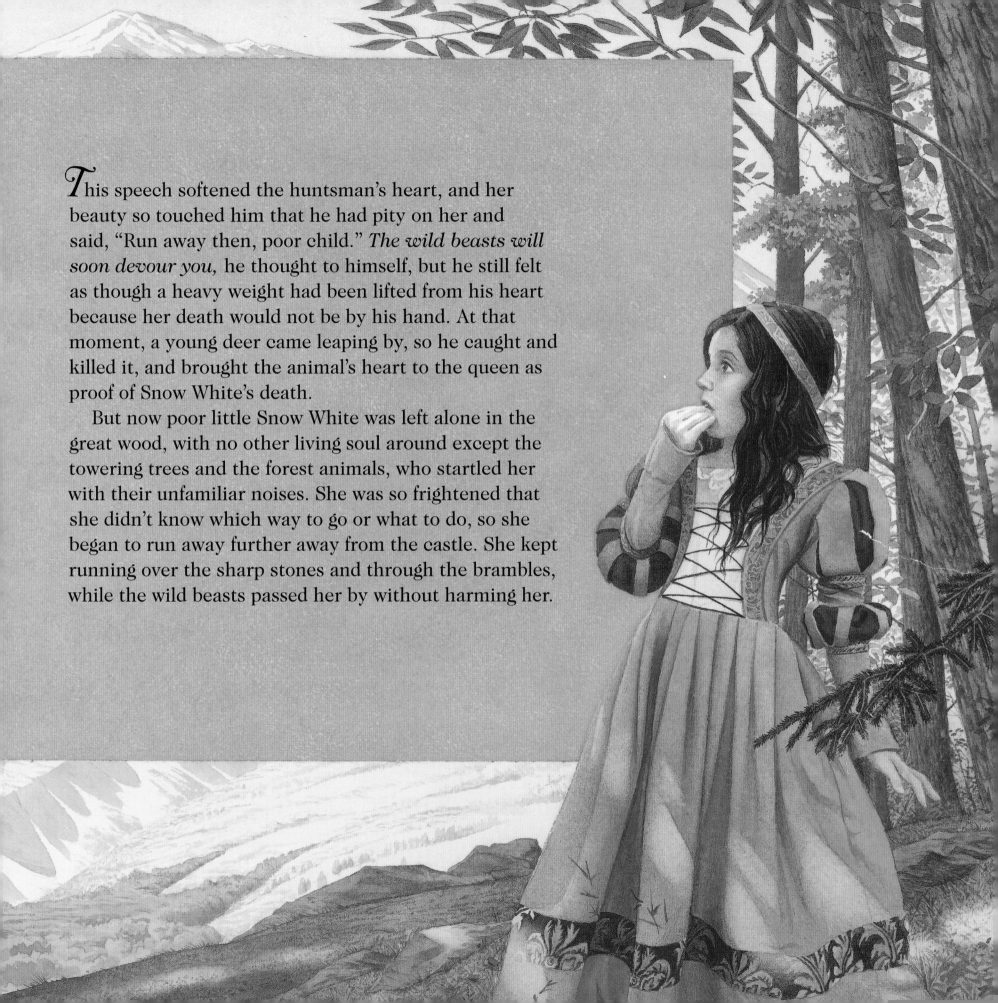

$\mathcal{T}$his speech softened the huntsman's heart, and her beauty so touched him that he had pity on her and said, "Run away then, poor child." *The wild beasts will soon devour you,* he thought to himself, but he still felt as though a heavy weight had been lifted from his heart because her death would not be by his hand. At that moment, a young deer came leaping by, so he caught and killed it, and brought the animal's heart to the queen as proof of Snow White's death.

But now poor little Snow White was left alone in the great wood, with no other living soul around except the towering trees and the forest animals, who startled her with their unfamiliar noises. She was so frightened that she didn't know which way to go or what to do, so she began to run away further away from the castle. She kept running over the sharp stones and through the brambles, while the wild beasts passed her by without harming her.

$\mathcal{S}$he ran as far as her feet could carry her until it was nearly dark. Then, just as she was about to fall from exhaustion, she saw a little house nestled in the forest, and she went inside to rest.

Everything was small inside the cottage, but very neat and clean. In the middle stood a little table covered with a white cloth. Snow White counted seven small plates full of food on the table, each with a spoon, knife, fork, and cup beside it. By the wall, seven little beds stood side by side, covered with clean white blankets and sheets.

Snow White was very hungry and thirsty, so she ate a little bit of the food from each plate, and drank a sip from each cup, for she did not want to eat up anyone's full meal.

Then, feeling very tired after her long run through the woods, she tried to lie down on one of the beds, but it was too short. The next one was too long, another too hard, and so on, until she tried the seventh bed, which was just right. And so she settled down on it and fell asleep.

When it became quite dark, the owners of the house returned home. They were seven dwarfs who had been working all day in the gold mines deep under the mountain. When they entered the house with their lanterns, they immediately noticed that someone had been there, for things were not as they had left them.

The first said, "Who has been sitting in my chair?"

The second said, "Who has been eating off my plate?"

The third said, "Who has been nibbling my bread?"

The fourth said, "Who has been eating my vegetables?"

The fifth said, "Who has been using my fork?"

The sixth said, "Who has been cutting with my knife?"

The seventh said, "Who has been drinking out of my cup?"

Then the first noticed a slight impression on his bed, and said, "Who has been lying on my bed?"

And the others came running and cried, "Someone has been on our beds, too!"

But when the seventh looked at his bed, he saw little Snow White lying there asleep. He called to the others, who cried out with astonishment as they gazed at the young girl.

"Goodness! What a beautiful child!" they said.

They were so delighted by her beauty that they did not wake her up, but left her asleep in bed. The seventh dwarf slept with his fellows, an hour at a time with each, until the night had passed.

When morning came, Snow White woke up and was quite frightened when she first saw the seven little men. But she relaxed when they were very kind to her and asked her name.

"I am called Snow White," she answered.

Then she told them how her stepmother had wished to get rid of her, how the huntsman had spared her life, and how she had run all day until she had found their little house.

When her tale was finished, the dwarfs said, "Will you stay with us and look after our household while we work in the mines? You may cook, make the beds, wash, sew, and knit, and keep everything neat and clean. We will make sure you have everything you need and keep you safe."

"Yes," said Snow White, "with all my heart."

And so she stayed with them and kept the house in order. Every morning they went to the mines under the mountain and dug for gold, and in the evening when they came home, Snow White had their supper ready for them.

But Snow White was to be left alone in the house all day long, so the good dwarfs warned her, saying, "Beware of your stepmother, who will soon learn that you are here. Don't let any one into the cottage when we are away."

Meanwhile, the queen, who thought that Snow White was dead, believed that she was now the most beautiful woman in the world. She stepped in front of her magic mirror and asked, "Mirror, mirror on the wall, Who is fairest of us all?"

The mirror replied, "The queen was fairest yesterday, But Snow White is fairer now, they say. The dwarfs protect her from your sway Within the forest, far away."

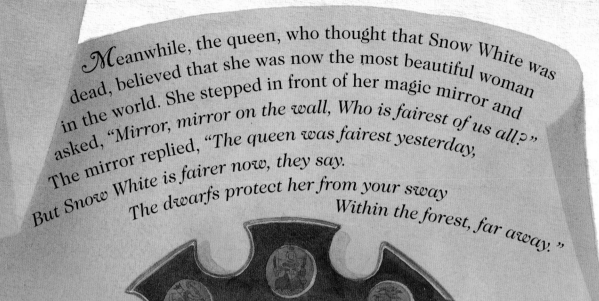

The queen was shocked and angry, for the mirror always spoke the truth, which meant that the huntsman had deceived her, and Snow White was still alive. She considered how she might make an end of Snow White, for as long as the queen was not the fairest in the land, her jealous heart left her no rest. At last she thought of a plan. She dressed up like an old peddler woman and used face paint to age herself, so that she would be quite unrecognizable. In this disguise, she crossed over the seven mountains to the home of the seven dwarfs.

She knocked at the door, calling, "Fine goods for sale! Beautiful goods for sale!"

Snow White peeped out of the window and said, "Good day, what have you got?"

"Fine goods, beautiful goods," answered the woman. "Dress lacing of every color."

I need not be afraid of letting in this good woman, thought Snow White, and she unbolted the door and bought a pretty length of lacing.

"This will go so beautifully with your dress," said the old woman. "Come and let me lace you up properly."

Suspecting nothing, Snow White allowed the old woman to lace her dress. But the old woman laced her up so quickly and tightly that it took Snow White's breath away, and she fell down as though she were dead.

"Now I am once more the most beautiful of all," the queen said to herself, as she hurried away.

Soon after the old woman left, the seven dwarfs came home. They were horrified when they saw their dear little Snow White lying motionless on the floor. They lifted her, and when they saw how tightly her dress was laced, they quickly cut the lacing in two. Slowly, she began to breathe again, and little by little she revived.

When the dwarfs heard what had happened, they said, "The old peddler woman was most likely the wicked queen in disguise! You must beware of letting anyone in when we are not here."

As soon as the wicked queen arrived home, she went to the magic mirror and asked,

"Mirror, mirror on the wall, Who is fairest of us all?"

And the mirror answered as before,

"The queen was fairest yesterday,
But Snow White is fairer now, they say.
The dwarfs protect her from your sway
Within the forest, far away."

The mirror's response enraged the queen, for she knew that Snow White was still alive. She thought to herself, *I must make something that will really put an end to her.* Using witchcraft, she made a poisoned comb. Then she disguised herself as a different old woman. She crossed the mountains and came to the home of the seven dwarfs, and knocked at the door, calling out, "Good wares to sell."

Snow White looked out of the window and said, "Go away, I must not let anyone in."

"But you may still look," answered the old woman, holding up the poisoned comb.

Snow White was so pleased with the comb that she opened the door.

"Now let me put the comb in your hair for you," said the old woman.

Poor Snow White, suspecting no evil, let the old woman do as she wished, but no sooner was the comb in her hair than the poison began to work, and the girl fell down unconscious.

"You paragon of beauty," cried the wicked queen as she left the dwarfs' house, "this is the end of you!"

Fortunately, it was nearly evening, and the seven dwarfs soon came home. When they saw Snow White lying on the ground as though she were dead, they immediately suspected her stepmother again. They quickly discovered the poisoned comb in her hair, and once they removed it, Snow White awoke and told them what had happened. They warned her once again to be on her guard, and to open the door for no one.

When the queen arrived home, she stood before her magic mirror and said,

> "Mirror, mirror on the wall,
> Who is fairest of us all?"

The mirror answered as before,

> "The queen was fairest yesterday,
> But Snow White is fairer now, they say.
> The dwarfs protect her from your sway
> Within the forest, far away."

When the queen heard those words again, she trembled and quivered with rage. "Snow White shall die," she said, "even if it costs me my own life." Then she went into a secret room, which no one ever entered but herself, and there she made a poisonous apple. The apple was so beautiful it would make anyone's mouth water, but one half of it was poisoned, and anyone who ate even a tiny bite of that side would instantly die.

When the apple was ready, the queen disguised herself like an old peasant woman and crossed the seven mountains to the dwarfs' home. When she knocked at the door, Snow White put her head out of the window and said, "I must not let anyone in; the seven dwarfs have forbidden me."

"It is all the same to me," said the peasant woman. "I can easily sell my apples elsewhere. But here, I will give you one before I go."

"No," answered Snow White, "I must not take anything."

"Are you afraid of poison?" laughed the woman. "Look here, I will cut the apple in half. You eat this side and I will eat the other." The woman split the apple into two pieces, taking a large bite from the safe portion as she secretly saved the poisonous half for the young girl.

Snow White longed to eat the beautiful apple, and when she saw the peasant woman eating safely, she stretched out her hand and accepted the other half. But no sooner had she taken a bite than she fell to the ground as if she were dead.

The queen laughed bitterly and said, "This time, surely the dwarfs will not be able to bring you to life again!"

When she arrived home, she once again asked the magic mirror,

"*Mirror, mirror on the wall,*
Who is fairest of us all?"

This time the mirror answered,

"*Queen, you are the fairest of them all.*"

Then her jealous heart was at rest, as much as a jealous heart can be.

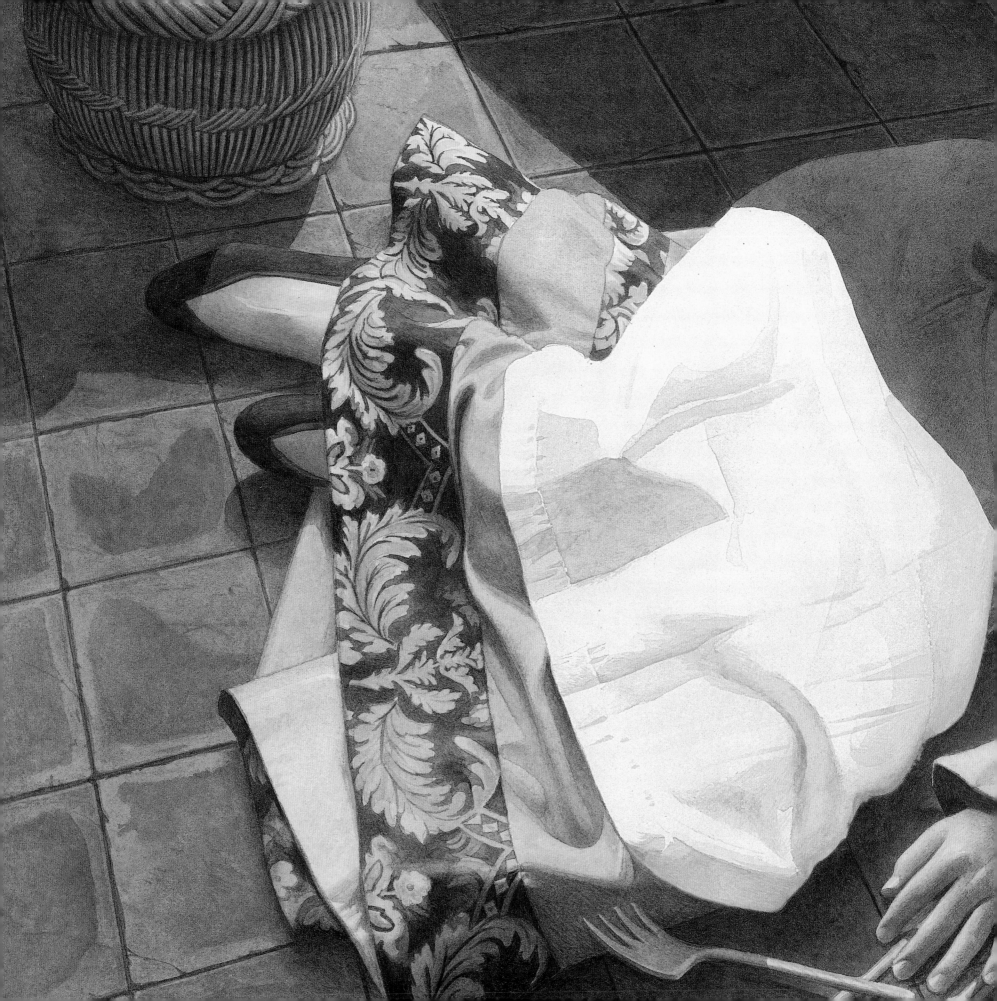

When the dwarfs returned home that evening, they found Snow White lying on the ground. Not a breath escaped her lips, and she seemed quite dead. They looked for poison, unlaced her dress, combed her hair, and washed her skin with water, but it was no use; the dear child did not awaken this time. They dressed her in white and placed her body on a long, flat stone, and all seven dwarfs mourned her for three full days. Then they prepared to bury her, but she still looked so fresh and lifelike, with beautiful rosy cheeks, that they said, "We cannot hide her away in the dark ground."

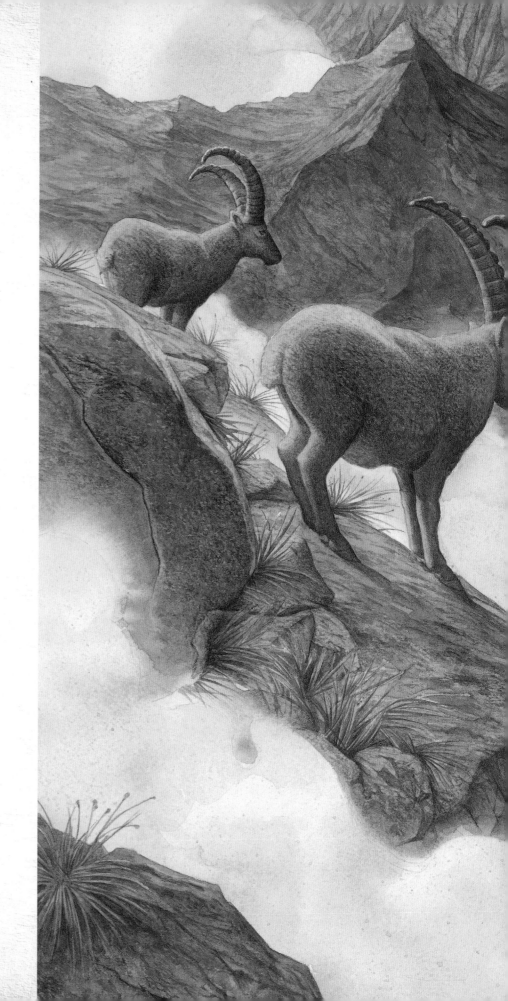

And so they had a coffin made of clear glass, so that she could be seen from every side, and they wrote her name on the top in gold letters. Then they placed the glass coffin up on the mountain, and one of them always remained by it to watch her. Even the birds came to mourn for Snow White, first an owl, then a raven, and last of all a dove.

For many years Snow White lay peacefully in her coffin, looking as though she were only asleep, for she was still as white as snow, as red as blood, and as black as ebony. One day, a prince was wandering in the wood and passed the night in the home of the seven dwarfs. When he saw Snow White lying within her glass coffin, he was stunned by her beauty. "Please let me have this coffin, and I will give you whatever you like for it," he begged the dwarfs.

But the dwarfs replied, "We will not sell it for all the gold in the world."

"Then give it to me as a gift," the prince said, "for I cannot live without Snow White, and I will honor and protect her as long as I live."

When the dwarfs saw that he cared so much for Snow White, they at last agreed to let him take her to his palace.

As his servants lifted the coffin to carry it down the mountain, they stumbled. As the coffin shook, the piece of poisoned apple fell out of Snow White's mouth, and she instantly awakened.

"Oh, dear! Where am I?" she asked. "Who are you?"

*T*he prince was full of joy to see Snow White revived. He said, "You are safe with me," and he told her all that had happened. Then he said, "I will love you better than all the world. Please come with me to my father's castle and become my wife."

Snow White agreed, and when they arrived, their wedding was celebrated with great splendor and magnificence.

Even Snow White's wicked stepmother was invited to the prince's wedding, but after she had dressed in her fine clothes to go, she stepped to her magic mirror and asked,

"Mirror, mirror on the wall,
Who is fairest of us all?"
The mirror answered,
"The queen was fairest yesterday;
The prince's bride is now, they say."
Upon hearing these words, the queen was furious. At first she was determined not go to the wedding, but then she felt she would have no peace until she had seen the prince's beautiful bride for herself. When she arrived and recognized that the bride was Snow White, she choked with rage and fear. To atone for her crimes, the evil queen was ordered to dance and dance while wearing heavy iron slippers, and she soon fell down from exhaustion and died.

Snow White and the prince lived and reigned happily over that land for many, many years, and sometimes they went up into the mountains to pay a visit to the little dwarfs who had been so kind to Snow White in her time of need.

ABOUT THE ILLUSTRATOR

Charles Santore is a renowned children's book illustrator whose work has been widely exhibited in museums and celebrated with recognitions such as the prestigious Hamilton King Award, the Society of Illustrators Award of Excellence, and the Original Art 2000 Gold Medal from the Society of Illustrators. He is best known for his luminous interpretations of classic children's stories such as the *New York Times* bestselling *The Night Before Christmas*, *The Little Mermaid*, *Snow White*, and *The Wizard of Oz*. Charles Santore lives and works in Philadelphia.

ABOUT APPLESAUCE PRESS

Good ideas ripen with time. From seed to harvest, Applesauce Press crafts books with beautiful designs, creative formats, and kid-friendly information on a variety of fascinating topics. Like our parent company, Cider Mill Press Book Publishers, our press bears fruit twice a year, publishing a new crop of titles each spring and fall.

Write to us at:

PO Box 454
Kennebunkport, ME 04046

Or visit us online at:
www.cidermillpress.com

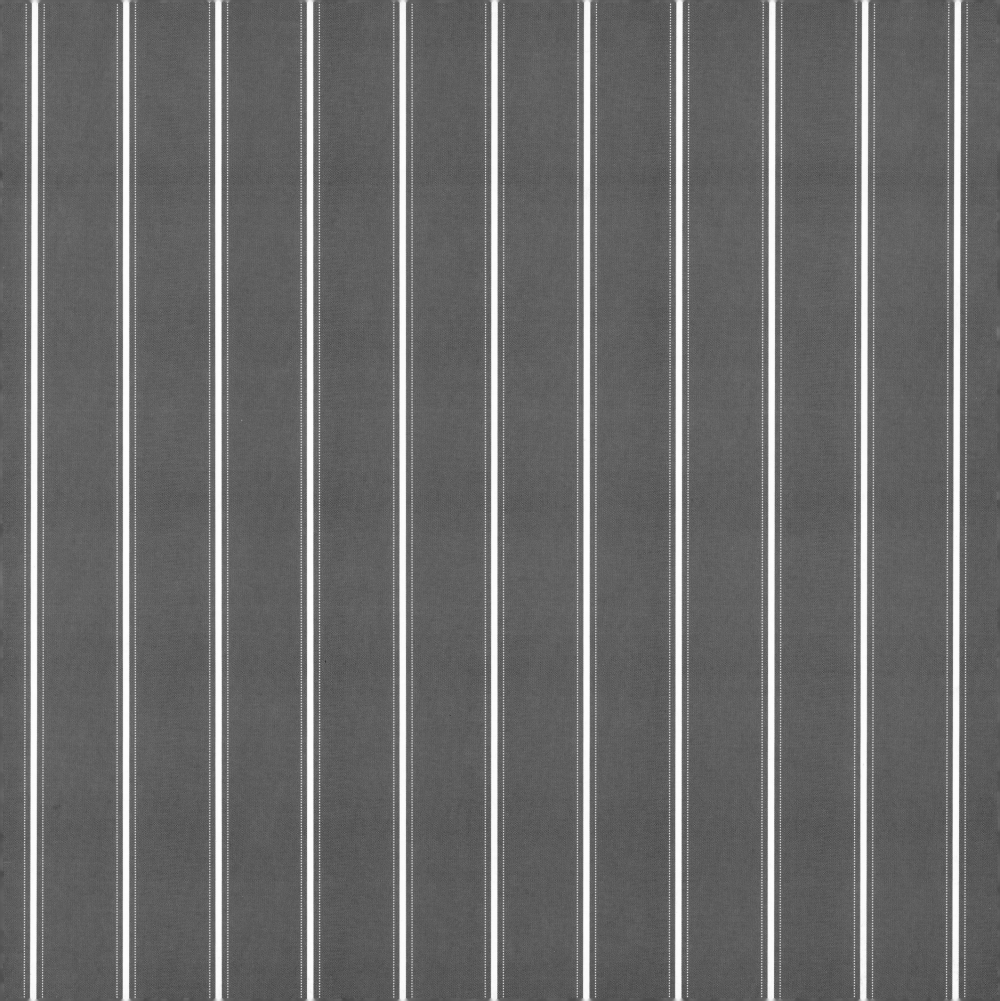

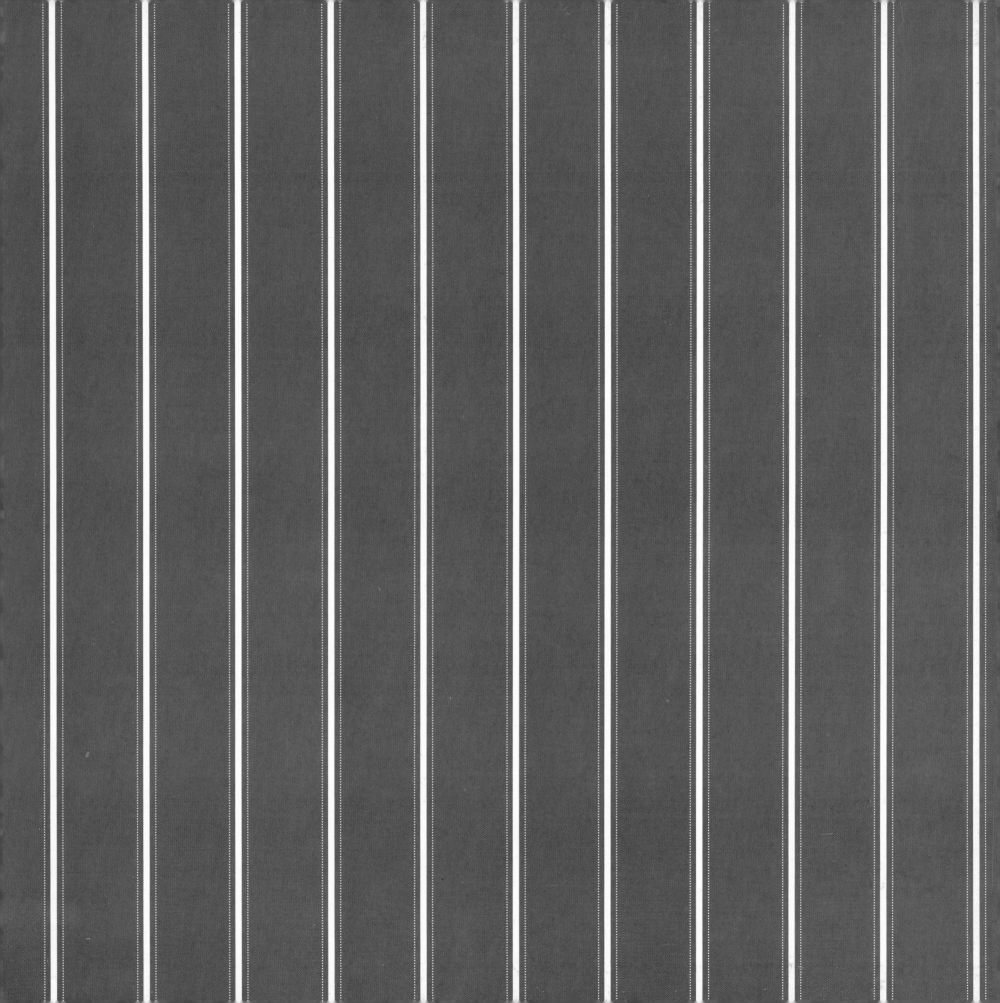